LITERARY LOVESTORIES

A Collection of 'How I Met...' Tales
from the County of Hertfordshire and Beyond

By Natasha Collins

Credits
Words by Natasha Collins
Illustrations by artist: Jordon Thompson
Cover and frames by graphic designer: Beverley Speight
Editing by Joanne Cetti
Inspired by interviews with:
Shauna, Julia, Bob, Priya, Dean, Deborah, Ian, Linda, Jeremy, Carole, Kevin, Anne, Lombardo, Charlotte, Luke, Lisa, Malcolm, Leigh, Nick, Helen, Nii, Abi, Paul, Laura, Salvatore, Gloria, Zak and Josephine.
Plus, the friend or family member which each couple nominated.

Prologue

My sincere and deepest thanks go to each couple who participated in this book. Their candidness was profoundly moving. As each couple recounted their 'how I met…' tale, it turned them into storytellers. In early 2015, I had sent a call-out for couples, to come forward and reveal their 'how I met…' tale to go in a collection book; a donation from each book sale going to Marriage Care, the relationship charity, to raise its profile. The idea came as one Marriage Care volunteer asked my husband and I, 'how did you meet?' The question came out of the blue and transported us back to a special, long-forgotten time.

Therefore it got me thinking that perhaps it might be nice to ask other people that same question, as a feel-good, reminiscing exercise. In addition, at around the same time, Middlesex University's supportive Enterprise Development Hub, part of the Business School, had assigned me a business mentor in the shape of Michaela Hopkins, a helpful, available and encouraging venture guru who said, 'why don't you create a book for family and friends to showcase your product offering?' (Literary Lifestories - turning life stories into literature).

Two little articles appeared in the press, one in Hertfordshire Life and another in the Hendon & Finchley and Barnet & Potters Bar Times. Also, BBC Three Counties Radio invited me into their studio to appear on the Nick Coffer show, where I announced the conception of Literary Lovestories, inviting the public to contact me with their story, to star in the book which would be published in time for Valentine's Day 2016.

Furthermore I approached couples that I knew. So my formula involved spreading the word locally. Nonetheless, an associate of mine saw my call-out, via the Association of Personal Historians and so she is featured with her love story, despite living in Tennessee, America. How could I say no to an additional love story? I decided to stick to 16 tales, to coincide and herald the 16th year of this current millennium.

I asked each couple the same set of questions, such as 'where did you go on your first date?' 'Describe your feelings at the time' and of course 'how did you meet?' Interviews took place either on the phone or via email or face to face. There was much laughter when recounting some tales, while others were philosophical as they described the moment their lives changed, sometimes after years of searching. It made me chuckle when couples politely disputed facts like anniversary dates with each other.

For added authenticity, each couple had put me in touch with someone who knew them well and I asked this friend / family member to describe what made the union-ship unique. The way each one gave thoughtful accounts was truly remarkable and I wanted to thank each one of them here. They know who they are.

Lastly, I contacted illustrator lecturers at Middlesex University's School of Art and Design, explaining that as a graduate from the School of Media and Performing Arts, and current PhD student in creative non-fiction, I was looking for an illustrator to help me tell the story of 16 real life couples. The artist's brief was to draw each couple's joint portrait from their favourite photo, for this true love story collection. Jordon Thompson (illustrator) and Beverley Speight (graphic designer) were sent my way. I hoped they were good. They proved to be outstanding. I hope that you too enjoy their work. Thank-you Jordon and Bev, you were both a pleasure to work with.

We need more positive narratives out there, in a world where negative storylines are given centre-stage. Despite it all, there are examples all around us of enduring, true love, keeping our societies together like the cement in the walls of a house. The love stories featured in this book are not necessarily shining examples of the best relationships, they are ordinary tales, a sample of coupledom across Hertfordshire and beyond. Hopefully this will inspire you to ask those questions of yourself or others.

Literary Lifestories is a service I set up in 2014, offering the public a chance to turn their life story into a biographical tale. *So often, this is the balm needed to understand and empathise - with a lived life.*

N.C.

Barnet, January 2016

Contents

Natasha Collins

Dedicated to my husband Cameron
and our daughter Pearl.

To all my family ~
thank-you so much for your love and support,
shown in everything you impart and do and in particular -
giving me the space and time to think and write.

One can pay back the loan of gold,
but one dies forever in debt to those who are kind.
Malayan Proverb

Thank-you too Jo!

Alex and Shauna

A lex and Shauna have always had that 'sparkle in the eye' for each other, revealing how much they enjoy being together. Alex - the tower of strength and Shauna - his compassionate support. They were married on the 31st October 2014 at St Mary the Virgin in Monken Hadley, Barnet. Alex has one child, Isabella, and the couple welcomed Oliver, their child together, in January 2016.

S hauna had always been an old fashioned girl at heart. Growing up with three brothers however, it was no wonder she developed a love of tomboy pursuits such as climbing trees, clay pigeon shooting and motorbikes. At heart however, she longed for a meaningful relationship with a kindly man and perhaps a family to call her own.

Shauna knew a thing or two about having a boyfriend. She had just come out of a relationship which lasted nearly a decade, but he wasn't her Mr Right and unbeknown to Shauna, she was about to meet 'the one'. In her spare time, Shauna was an online moderator for a motorcycling forum. One day she decided to write a post, unrelated to motorcycling, seeking advice about a new television she had just purchased. Immediately she spotted a new chap online, Alex, who replied to her question and they started a conversation. 'I like the look of this bloke,' she thought. He then invited her out for a coffee at the haven for North London motorcyclists, known as the Ace Café on the North Circular Road.

Feeling excited, she went along and ordered a tea. Alex also ordered a tea and they sat chatting away. They decided to head down to Soho, as many motorcyclists did on a Friday night. However, she made a discreet phone call to one of her trusted confidantes, 'if I pick you up on the way, please be my chaperone, I'd love to know what you think'. That night Shauna's friend gave her the 'thumbs up'.

The couple have been inseparable ever since. Sometime after this first date, Shauna's friend remarked, 'I never hear from you anymore, Shauna, you two are like a pair of love birds, those stolen smiles, secret caresses, private jokes'. 'Yes, we're very close and loving to each other,' replied Shauna.
'Do I hear wedding bells?'
'Well, as you know, Alex's first marriage didn't go to plan, so understandably he's not keen, and he has his young daughter to think about too.'

A few more years went by and not only had their love grown deeper, they still found comfort in each other's company, so Shauna planned to ask Alex to marry her, on Valentine's Day, 2013. However the day didn't go well. Alex's train home was delayed, it was raining heavily and just like that, the 'right moment' was quashed. Nonetheless, by Christmas Eve that same year, Alex was ready to ask the same question.

Together with his daughter, he presented Shauna with a large box. Shauna tore the paper only to find another box, then another. Ten boxes later she came to the smallest one with a message 'there's still time to run', but she didn't run, she cried as Alex went down on one knee and asked her to be his wife.

A few months into their relationship, Shauna had discovered that Alex didn't drink tea but at the Ace Café that night, he saw Shauna with a tea, and he could think of nothing else.

Andreas and Julia

A ndreas and Julia hold a genuine fondness for each other, which is evident to
anyone in their company. The way they behave and the things they say to each
other demonstrate this affection. Together they are easy going and are an oasis of
calm with each other. They have been together since November 2013.

I t was February 2013 and Julia was due to return to her part-time job in
tele-customer services, a post she held at weekends. When the day arrived,
Julia was feeling tearful. She hadn't left her baby girl once, in all the seven
months that had gone by since Sasha's birth the previous summer.

Alas, time goes on, and babies need their mothers that little bit less. This was
no consolation for Julia; leaving her baby, she felt sad. At the same time she
was nervous at the prospect of returning to the job. Would she still remember
how everything worked, having spent the best part of a year nursing
her beautiful baby?

"Julia, come and meet Andreas, he only started a few months back,' came a colleague's voice. Julia was not in the mood for making first impressions, but more importantly than this, she didn't want the new guy to think she was an emotional wreck.

'Hi, I'm Andreas', the new fellow said, with an outstretched hand, a beaming smile and a look which told Julia, 'you're going to be ok, I'm not going to judge you'. 'Welcome back to the fold!' he continued. Julia laughed so much that day, something she had forgotten how to do. Reflecting later at home, she knew they would be friends for life.

Months later, Andreas came to collect her for their first date, looking smart in a stylish shirt and trousers and smelling good. Julia was in her favourite, floaty red dress and heels. What followed was a long drive, chatting and laughing together. Having now entered a local high street, Andreas suggested, 'Perhaps we should go somewhere to eat?'

'Can you imagine if we went to KFC for our first date?' Julia exclaimed in mock dismay.

'Yes I can, Andreas laughed and pulled into the drive-through. Two chicken-wraps and bucket of pop-corn chicken later, Julia quietly noted how easy and comfortable things were between them. It appeared they both wanted to spend time in each other's company and it didn't matter where.

The road trips continued and with them came a song which kept coming on the radio, Naughty Boy's La La La, featuring Sam Smith, which became their little anthem. Years later the song would always be linked to those happy car journeys.

'How would you like to come to Cyprus?' asked Andreas one day.

'Really?' replied Julia. 'You want to take me to Cyprus?'

'Yes, Protaras to be exact, you will love it!'

A few months later, a bemused Julia asked, 'Why are we travelling to the airport the day before?' The answer became clear when Andreas pulled into the Marriott Heathrow, and checked into a runway-view room. The pair spent the evening watching the planes take-off and land, while tucking into dinner via room service. Julia did love Cyprus. It was a romantic break in the sunshine which she needed. At the same time Julia learned all about Andreas' culture.

Bob and Priya

Bob and Priya run relationship counselling workshops and are accepting and open and this helps put the couples they counsel at their ease. The two are relaxed about all aspects of the body and share a passion for reconciling. They were married on the 22nd October 2001 at Harbin Hot Springs in California. Bob has one child, Adam, and one grandchild, Dade. Priya has two children, Andy and Julia.

All alone on the plane to California, Priya sat back and day-dreamed about the workshop she was about to embark on, set at a natural spring resort. She, a psychotherapist ran American-inspired couples workshops in London, and was heading off to experience the latest offering, titled Sexuality and Spirituality.

It was all very exciting. Priya had never been to the States before and she was passionate about love in relationships, connecting and intimacy. It was August

1999 and although Priya was not on the look-out for love in any way, this was about to change. During the workshop, Priya thought she would indulge and make the most of the warm, hot tub, when a fun and friendly stranger joined her. There was an instant attraction between the two and Priya couldn't ignore the feeling of something special.

When Priya returned to London, her new cuddly friend followed a few weeks later. His name was Bob and he was just as smitten. Bob thought he would come to see how the UK workshop was going, with the major incentive of seeing Priya again.

Priya was delighted to see Bob again and as time went by, thought about him as a possible new partner. However the 6000 miles between them frightened her. Confiding in a friend one day, Priya revealed her anxieties. Her friend replied, 'look, it's 6000 miles, you're not keen on living in America because of your family here in the UK, so you can stop it now, Priy!'.

Priya laughed as she revealed, 'the thing is, Jane, something tells me that I've embarked on something special and I'm reluctant to let it go so soon.' Over the next two years the couple tried to be together as much as possible and the longest they were apart was nine weeks.

While over in California, Priya caught a cold and between sniffling and coughing in bed, Bob brought her a soup and confessed, 'Priya, I don't have all the answers. All I know is that I do not want this long period in between trips anymore. I want to spend the rest of my life with you. I know that we still have no idea where we're going to live but… will you marry me?'

Priya accepted, not knowing where they were going to live – California or London? Both were hesitant in leaving their home country, yet both were unwilling to give up their second chance of happiness, which they had found in each other. Once married, Bob succumbed and moved to Barnet.

The couple began leading couples workshops together in the UK, helping couples to connect and become more intimate. Together they formed
Intimacy Works, offering workshops for improving connection and communication.

Dean and Alison

Dean and Alison have had their fair shares of life's challenges, causing Dean to be an unhappy soul at times. But Alison proved to be an extremely supportive partner winning his love time and time again. They were married on the 6th October 2001 at Dunstable Registry Office. They have Megan, Dean's child from a previous relationship and another child together, Taylor,

The entire world was gripped by media speculation that all digital systems would lose their data upon the stroke of midnight on the 31st of December 1999, otherwise known as 'the millennium bug'. Engineering technicians such as Dean were in especially high demand around mid-December of that year, as they waded through the work load and struggled to keep up with call outs.

Dubbed 'the ogre' at the company he was a manager at, no one dared approach his office door unless it was a matter of life or death. With the added pressure of the Millennium Bug, Dean's co-workers could feel the 'keep out' vibes.

So when Dean heard a faint knock at his door, he glared at his clock and noted the time was 15:12. Frustrated, he bellowed, 'YES!' On the other side of the door, was the bravest team member from the service desk, Matthew. With a sinking feeling Matthew opened the door and blurted, 'I know you're really busy, Mr Dean, but we have a client in tears. She's trying to do the Christmas wage run for about 300 employees but she's spilt lime juice all over her keyboard and now it's not working.'

There was no getting out of it, Dean would have to go. With that thought, he got up, grabbed a spare keyboard from the cupboard and stormed off. Dean got in his van and made his way to the address.

When Dean arrived at the premises, he was still very much in a bad mood. He walked in reception and gave his name. He was met by Alison. As Dean followed her along the corridor to her office, something changed, his hardened heart began to soften, as Alison's swaying hips hypnotised this 'ogre' so that he resembled something of a love-struck puppy.

As Dean swapped the keyboard and Alison went off to make him a tea, one of the Directors, her boss, walked in the room. Dean found himself asking the man, 'I'm not normally so forward, but I have to ask, is Alison single?'

'Yes, she is.' The two men smiled and exchanged light hearted, male banter, which was brought to an abrupt end when Alison re-entered with the cup of tea. The Director left the room and half an hour later Dean was still there, in Alison's office, chatting away. Upon leaving he gave her his email address, his phone number and added, 'do call me'.

With Christmas and New Year out of the way, Alison called Dean. Four weeks later, Dean asked for Alison's hand in marriage. The following year, the couple tied the knot and a few years after, had a daughter.

Alison proved to be Dean's rock. She nursed his dying parents at home and when redundancy loomed, threatening them with the prospect of downsizing, to his dismay Alison just shrugged and said, 'it doesn't matter, we'll sell the house'. Years later Alison told him, 'you've always been grumpy - but I love a grump to cuddle at night!'

Evert and Deborah

Evert and Deborah were two wondering, lost souls, searching in all directions for the missing piece of life's puzzle. When they found each other, the couple's love could be felt in the hearts of all around them. They were married on the 23rd March 2006 in Davidson County, Tennessee. Evert has one child, Thijs and Deborah has one child, Brewer, and one grandchild.

The year was 2004 and Deborah was getting ready to attend the Americana Music Conference in Nashville. The writer was covering the event for a music magazine and her task was to interview the many musicians. However, little did Deborah know that she would be interviewing her third chance at love, and would it really be the guy who kept disappearing whenever she entered a room?

His name was Evert, the owner of a record label called CoraZong Records, who was there promoting a band called, Burrito Deluxe. However, upon meeting, he appeared rude as he did his best to avoid the writer. In fact he fled whenever she was in a room conducting an interview. 'Not to worry', thought Deborah, as her best smile waned, with the burden of the wound. 'Plenty more fish in the sea,' she reassured herself. It was the last night of the conference, and with all the toe-tapping music being played, Deborah was very much in a dancing mood. Realising no one wanted to dance, she surveyed the room and saw one head bopping up and down. It belonged to 'mr escape man' Evert.

Suddenly the DJ, Tony Joe White, played 'Polk Salad Annie' and Deborah couldn't resist, she fought her way through the crowd. 'Would you like to dance?' she asked. Evert replied, 'yes'. For the next ten minutes the two danced; ten unforgettable minutes. Little did Deborah know that a flame had ignited in this stranger's heart the moment he saw her, but she would never have guessed from his actions up until that point.

After that first dance they both went back to their separate seats and it wasn't until three months later that Evert phoned Deborah and invited her to dinner. He had kept her business card, given at their first encounter. Now it was Evert's turn to do the chasing. He sent her a love song from Europe every day after that first dinner. Evert was from the Netherlands. Many songs she had never heard before, like P.P.Arnold's 'Life is But Nothing'. He even proposed marriage to her with every song. But Deborah didn't take him seriously.

It wasn't until Evert threw his wedding ring into the sea that Deborah realised he was ready to end his unhappy union and try again at happiness. The pair were engaged for a year, during which, Deborah asked Evert, 'are we doing the right thing?' He reassured her, 'we are, we are seizing our final chance of happiness'.

The couple tied the knot and Deborah wept all through their vows. Evert went on to lose his retirement savings as a result of his break-up but he was back in touch with his mother and old friends again and so the price was worth the new life he was given.
Years later he told her, 'I felt the hand of God on my shoulder and a voice told me 'you're going to marry that girl'.
'So that's why you kept disappearing,' Deborah deduced, with a detective's hindsight.

Ian and Linda

Ian and Linda have been loving and committed to each other for 60 years. They were married on the 26th May 1956 at St Barnabas Church in Finchley. They have three children: Helen, Neil and Duncan, and nine grandchildren.

Ian was crestfallen. The year was 1954, he was 20 years old and he had just broken up with his girlfriend. However, this was not the main reason he felt gloomy; he had his work dinner and dance coming up and now he had no date.

Meanwhile, a 19-year-old named Linda, from nearby Finchley, was making her way to High Barnet's Whalebones in Wood Street for the customary Thursday night gathering of the 18/30 club. Linda made the journey each week. Linda worked in London during the week but enjoyed the locality and friendships formed at the Whalebones.

Ian was also a member of this youth club. Members enjoyed the social life it gave them, the opportunity to meet people of the same age and tennis on a Tuesday and Sunday afternoon. There was always a weekend activity planned and table-tennis was also a regular fixture. A Miss Cowing owned the property and would let-out the stable rooms to local groups for community purposes, including the 18/30 Club.

Ian was not a keen dancer but he did want to attend his work function. The event was on his mind that evening and he mentioned it to his friend during a car journey home when suddenly Linda who happened to be travelling in the same car said, 'I'll come if you like. I'll keep you company'.

Ian was jolly pleased to finally have a partner to go with him and Linda was content to have an evening out, later confiding in a friend, 'I think Ian's a pleasant enough chap'. The pair soon became an item and took their first holiday together to Jersey, with Linda's sister and brother-in-law. The following year the couple got engaged and on the 26th May 1956, Ian and Linda celebrated their wedding day at St Barnabas Church in Finchley and later at the Red Lion in High Barnet.

The pair decided to go to Betws-y-Coed in Wales for their honeymoon, with a tour along the way. Stopping at the Swan Hotel in Stratford, they were shocked to discover their reservation had been cancelled. A group of American tourists had descended on the area and needed accommodation. 'Sorry Sir, it should have been made clearer to you, but you had to arrive before dinner at 6pm, and so we have now re-let your room. But we'll phone another local hotel for you.'

The following morning they awoke in a county-side hotel, far from the town. Having eventually found a pub for lunch, they were a good five miles into their journey towards Wales when Linda cried, 'Ah, my ring! I must have left it at the pub!'

They turned round and once back at the pub, they saw it had closed for the afternoon. The two banged at the door. Luckily someone was still about and let them in, 'Has a ring been found? I've lost my wedding ring,' gasped Linda. She searched the cloakroom and eventually found it in the roller towel.

Jeremy and Carole

Jeremy and Carole are the kind of couple who know they are very lucky to have met. Setting a high standard for their children to follow, yet being far from perfect either. The couple choose to be together rather than needing to. They were married on the 21st August 1977 at the Old Farm Avenue synagogue in Southgate. They have two children, Yael and Shai and two grandchildren, Xander and Alice.

Nestled in the heart of the Finchley Road in north London used to stand a house where a group of young and beautiful things lived communally. It was the 1970s, and the group were part of a youth movement, still living the true spirit of 1960s London, sharing what little they had with each other and where a cup of tea welcomed everybody.

A comforting brew was certainly what Jeremy needed when he wandered into the house one cold, November night, feeling lost and unloved. The 21-year-old had just broken up with his girlfriend, and his Saturday nights were usually spent with her. Sitting on the couch in the living room, Jeremy spotted a whole host of familiar faces as he tried his best to be sociable.

'Hi, I'm Carole!' Jeremy turned and saw a girl, about his age, whom he had seen pottering about before. 'Hi, I'm Jeremy,' he replied to the friendly and attractive stranger. 'And if I look miserable, it's because I am.' Jeremy felt so at ease in Carole's company that he found himself pouring out his heart.

While Carole suggested some mutual, single friends who might suit him, Jeremy took note but very soon thought, 'I wouldn't mind seeing more of you'. Like magnets, the pair began arranging to see each other all the time. Jeremy was a student and Carole had only just started her first job, so they tended to go round to each other's homes. Their first date was one of Carole's babysitting duties.

About a month later, Jeremy was invited to a party hosted by Carole's parents. Carole's grandmother took a shine to him and announced, 'I'm going to give Jeremy something because he's lovely'. She then took his hand and put a five pound note in it.

When the New Year came round, Carole reminded Jeremy about his travel plans which were due to begin that September. Carole was honest, 'will you remain faithful?' she asked. Jeremy too answered honestly, 'I'm a young man with needs, Carole.' Carole then blurted it out, 'well, will you marry me then, and I'll come with you?' Jeremy looked in wonder and replied without hesitating, 'yes Carole, I will'.

Spring came, and while organising their wedding, which was due to take place that summer, they took Jeremy's motorbike and visited beautiful Kew Gardens. On another trip, heading towards Cornwall on the M4, the motorbike broke down and Carole's father, in his cab, came to tow them back to Jeremy's family home in Ealing. They had to take Carole's family car instead and eventually spent an enriching time, camping on the coast, without the hustle and bustle of friends.

Remarkably, if someone had told them at the time that after children and grandchildren, the couple's relationship would be better than it ever was and that in their 60s, they believed the best was still to come, well, they would have fallen off their bike!

Kevin and Anne

Kevin and Anne's connection is one of pure love. Each is a free spirit yet show appreciation for the sacred bond they share. They creatively celebrate their love each day and were married on the 21st December, 2012 in Camden's Town Hall. The couple then went to Morocco for a sacred ceremony in the desert under the stars. Their first child, Phoenix, was born in May 2015.

Anne decided to leave LA's Venice Beach, which had been her home for too long. The Swedish young woman had her heart set on being a war photographer, based somewhere in Europe. So Anne boldly purchased her ticket for Iraq and was left with a few weeks to fill, so she chose to spend the time in London. All was to going to plan. Anne was to stay with a friend in the capital city, hopefully fitting in a road trip across Europe.

Anne was on a mission to find herself and travel would be the restoring remedy needed on the journey. Anne thought that it might be handy to know a few more people in England's hub so she found herself browsing MySpace, an early, online social network, this was after all, 2005.

She spotted a profile picture which immediately seized her attention, 'Kevin. He used to be a chef and is now a technical architect. He seems really nice!' she surmised. 'I'm going to send him a message. Besides, I might need help with my website.'

Once Anne landed in London, she went to find the friend she had planned to stay with, so that she could unpack and start sightseeing. Kevin soon called and they arranged to meet in a bar called The Couch in Soho. 'Hi, is that you Anne?' 'Yes it's me. Hi Kevin! I've started already' 'That's ok, I don't drink,' Kevin replied smiling. Anne was embarrassed, but it didn't last long, Kevin put her at ease and the two moved onto Camden and then Hampstead Heath. Anne later reflected, 'it's as though I've met my best friend'.

The two met up again, this time in Highbury & Islington for breakfast. Kevin had brought Anne an A to Z of London to help her navigate the tube system. Anne poured her heart out. She revealed that her 'friend' turned out to be a foe because he had asked her to sleep with him in order to continue staying at his flat. Kevin listened and wanted to help her in any way he could.

Kevin offered to put her up. 'It's only for a couple of days,' she assured him. 'It's absolutely fine,' Kevin replied. A few days turned into a few months and a few months turned into a few years and Kevin was in love.

Anne on the other hand was on a quest to find herself and wasn't ready for true love. 'It's so weird, but if we met years from now – I'd be ready,' Anne confessed.

The two were always honest with each other. Kevin understood and after three years Anne was ready for a trip to advance her development – Jordan. Kevin, ever patient – bought her the ticket, selling his beloved vinyls, knowing he might never see her again.

Anne was in Jordan and missed her best friend whom she had grown to love deeply. After a few months, Anne returned to London to be with Kevin.

Lombardo and Charlotte

Lombardo and Charlotte are described as a fiery couple who are in love. Their union-ship is defined by laughter and seeing the funny side in situations. They are always ready to lend a hand and despite the meeting of two cultures – it works. They were married on the 28th August 2005 at Our Lady of Lourdes in Arnos Grove. They have two children, Julian Joseph and Claudia Elisabetta.

'Tell me your life story in five minutes,' Charlotte asked the dark-haired stranger. She liked this chat-up line and judging by the smile on the handsome young man's face, so did he. Ten minutes earlier, Charlotte and her friends had spotted a group of good looking boys, by the bar in Epping Forest Country Club, and they had placed bets on who could pull who.

Charlotte had always fancied Italians. Just ten years earlier, in 1987, Madonna had immortalised the 'Italians Do It Better' slogan t-shirt, which she wore in her video - Papa Don't Preach. At the end of the night, when her quarry wrote down his number for her, she thought he had made up a name, '

'Lom-bar-do,' she read out loud, 'write your real name, it must be Gary or something'. But, as Charlotte was about to find out, she had bagged herself a full-blooded Italian man, albeit one who was brought-up in Ponders End.

For their first date, Charlotte had invited Lom (as he was affectionately known) to the Hickstead Dressage Ball, a prestigious horse-associated event. Charlotte was excited to have Lom there as her date. She admired the way Lom convincingly pretended to know all about horses.
There was a prominent Lord at the Ball, and after an evening of frivolous chit chat, he collapsed onto a chair next to Lombardo. Lom looked equally shattered, as he thought out loud, 'I really fancy a beer'. The Lord then got up, disappeared for five minutes and came back with two beers, one for Lom and one for himself; truly a result in the champagne-quaffing venue.

Lom and Charlie (as she was affectionately known) continued dating. Lom wanted to wait a while before introducing his new girlfriend to his parents. But that didn't last long. Coming home from a date one day, Lom's mother asked him, 'who's the blond girl?' Behind her was Lom's sister holding a video cassette. They'd seen images of Lom, earlier in the day, hand in hand with Charlotte at the Italian Church in Clerkenwell, enjoying the annual procession. The pair had gone there and so had BBC's TV news.

The following year, the couple welcomed Julian into the world and when their boy was about six years old, Lom went to buy an engagement ring, with a view to asking Charlotte to marry him. However, the surprise was foiled, as Julian blurted out, 'mum, will you marry dad?'
Charlotte said 'yes' and the wedding plans were on their way.
A honeymoon was booked, a continuation of 'meeting the family' in Campodimele, Italy. The night before the wedding, Charlotte was nervous. She phoned Lom at work, the receptionist replied, 'you want to speak to my Lomby? I'll just get him for you'. Charlotte, in her fragile state of pre-wedding nerves was furious. Lom tried his best to diffuse the situation.

The couple went on to have another child, a girl, they named Claudia, completing the family. Charlotte had won the bet, placed in a long forgotten night club, just outside Chigwell, all those years ago.

Luke and Lisa

Luke and Lisa share fundamental qualities, which keep them together, such as their loving, generous and caring natures. They work hard at keeping their union a positive and happy one by supporting one another. The respect they show each other is shown in the space they give one another to grow - both as individuals and as a couple. They have been together since May 2001 and have a son called Gino.

The year was 1994 and Luke was 17 years old. One day, his best friend Sally took Luke to see her older sister, who lived in a shared house. One of the house mates was Lisa. Upon seeing her he thought, 'she's lovely, what a beautiful smile'.

However, Lisa was older than him and so the attraction was not reciprocated, in fact she barely noticed him. The next time their paths crossed was at a New Year's Eve party, about four years later. The two began talking and got on well. Another four years went by and the pair spotted each other at a friend's house party. Luke had heard that Lisa had just broken up with someone and so did not want to pressurise her but his friends goaded him, 'go on Luke, chat her up!'

The group of friends uncomfortably stayed the night, all in one room. The following day, Luke asked Lisa, 'could I have your number?' Upon Luke's request, Lisa scratched her phone number, with her key, onto the nearest bit of paper she could fine, a dirty cigarette packet.

Luke texted the next day but heard nothing. A couple of weeks later he phoned the number and an old lady answered. He realised, that in her hurry, Lisa had given him the wrong number. He asked his friend Sally for Lisa's number. He called Lisa and asked her out. They dated, fell in love and for three months were devoted to one another.

However, Luke had travels ahead of him. Luke's private feelings about it were, 'if things between Lisa and I work out. I'm going to be with her for the rest of my life; so I must go travelling now so that I have some life experience behind me'.

Lisa received text messages, photos and emails for months nonstop. Until one day, Luke was stuck in a remote part of Laos and in 2002, internet connection was still a thing of the future. By the time Luke reached Sydney, he headed for the nearest phone box to call Lisa. Lisa said, 'I think it's best if you don't call me for a while'.

Luke had understood that while he couldn't 'stoke the fire' it had fizzled, and there was probably another man in his place. He was heartbroken. Eventually he managed to convince her to come to Canada, the last leg of the tour. When Lisa arrived she was still confused and so they spent a month as friends. It was the last day of their trip and they were now in New York. At a restaurant Lisa ordered a burger and chips. As she began to tuck in, she looked across to Luke and then asked him how many chips he wanted.

Years later she confessed that his answer touched her so profoundly, it was then that she knew Luke was 'the one' for her. He had replied, 'four'. The concept of being content with just four of her chips made her giggle till her ribs hurt.

Malcolm and Leigh

Malcolm and Leigh decide to embrace life together and as a result have formed a deep, loving and honest bond. They help those around them, such as giving advice to other couples at their Church. They were married on the 17th February 1996 at St Barnabas Church in North Finchley. They have three children, Jonathan, Libby and Daniel.

Malcolm first spied Leigh at a Dickensian carol concert in the mid-1990s. There was something about her that caught his imagination. It might have had something to do with the Victorian frock Leigh had on, about two sizes too small and complete with bonnet.

He next saw her about four months later at a large group gathering, all making their way to Spaghetti Opera in London's Fleet Street to celebrate a birthday. He remembered that Leigh was the girl at the concert and once they were in the restaurant, he made sure that he sat opposite her.

'So, did you go to University?' he asked while snapping a breadstick.
'I did, yes,' replied Leigh.
'Great, what year?'
'Year? I think I graduated about five years ago now. Wait a minute... you're trying to figure out how old I am?'

Malcolm was indeed trying to work out the young woman's age without directly asking her. Next came the singing. In order to appear well versed in Opera, he made a request for a particular aria from La Boheme.
The Opera singer in question became somewhat animated during the piece, standing behind the diners, running her hands over their shoulders. When she got to Malcolm, she stopped, as she sang at the top of her voice and at the pivotal moment, she put her hands either side of his head, pulled it back into her bosom and gave it a good shake. Leigh looked on, not believing her eyes, and Malcolm? He just continued talking to Leigh. He thought to himself, 'best to ignore what's happening'.
After the puzzling moment had passed, while their friends were falling about in fits of laughter, Leigh remarked, 'you were totally unfazed, as though it happens to you all the time!'

Soon after, a barn dance was planned by the group, and because Leigh had been taking Ceroc lessons with a male friend, she took the opportunity practise a few moves. However, she didn't expect to remain dancing the entire night. Malcolm was there, and not to be outdone by the Ceroc-dancing companion, asked Leigh to dance each time the two finished their dance.

The pair soon became an item. Leigh thought this was going to be a passing thing but a moment shortly came when Malcolm looked at her in a way that no man had ever looked at her before. Things were getting serious. And when Malcolm referred to shared, future plans, it occurred to Leigh that perhaps she had already met 'the one'.
'If Malcolm should ever propose, that's the ring I want,' Leigh confided to a colleague while peering through a glass cabinet at London's Silver Vaults one lunch-time at work. Three days later, after a curry in West Hampstead (with a number of failed 'will you... pass the salt' moments) Malcolm got down on one knee in West End Lane and asked Leigh to be his wife.

Nick and Helen

Nick and Helen's union was written in the stars. They eventually found each other and are the best of friends who support each other completely and selflessly. The couple were married on the 18th December 1999 at the Holy Trinity Church in Barnet. They have two boys, Ben and Luke. Plus, Helen's eldest son, Adam, is now married.

It was a sunny, early Spring day when Nick decided to tidy his front garden and do a spot of weeding. Lost in his thoughts he was beginning to come to terms with the fact that his relationship with a Somerset lady was over; at heart he was a Barnet boy - born and bred. Nevertheless he was conscious that the following year he was going to be celebrating his 40th birthday.

'Hello,' came a kindly voice from over the front gate. Nick looked up and was astonished to see… Helen. 'Hi' was all that Nick could say. Undeterred, Helen went on, 'I live in that house there with my son'. Helen was pointing to the house next to Nick's neighbour. 'Pleased to meet you,' Nick replied politely.

Over the course of the next few months the pair happily struck up conversations whenever they saw each other. In time Nick told Helen, 'I know who you are but you don't know who I am, do you?' Judging from Helen's confused expression she didn't. Nick gave his full name and the penny dropped; they were children together, their mums had been in the same babysitting circle.

They shared the same friends growing up, were in the same youth club and went to the same Church. Helen plucked up the courage to ask him out, 'you're an odd one, come to a quiz night with me?' and Nick accepted.

On the 1st of April 1999, the pair planned to go on their first proper date to the Vue cinema in Finchley to see Shakespeare in Love. During the dinner beforehand at an American diner, Nick felt at ease, happy and intrigued by Helen. 'Oh this is good,' he thought to himself. The film was sold out, so they settled for another, but left early to continue their conversation.

On their second date, Nick was burning with a question that he felt he just had to ask. At the risk of sounding bold, given their ages, he summoned the nerve to ask, 'Helen, are you prepared to have children?' Now, put on the spot, Helen paused before answering. 'If I met someone, fell in love, got married – then yes, I would want children.' Nick was blissfully happy with the answer.

The couple married in the December of that year at the Holy Trinity Church in Lyonsdown Road, with Helen's son as ring bearer and Nick's brother as best man. They held a 'bring and share' reception and Helen became pregnant about a year and a half afterwards with Ben, their first child. Luke followed the following year. Sometime afterwards, Helen's parents came round with a surprise. 'What is it?' asked Helen excitedly. Her mum handed Nick and Helen an old photograph. 'Can you spot each other in the group of infants?'

Sure enough there was Nick in one corner and his future wife on the other side. They had lived parallel lives without ever fully interacting until the time was right, that year before the new millennium.

Nii and Abi

Nii and Abi are described as 'a super special' couple. They are well-suited and their differing personalities complement each other. They give one another strength and hope to deal with everyday life. Their wedding day was the 21st April 2007 at All Saints Pastoral Centre, London Colney, St Albans. They have three children, Dijani, Amari and Nala.

Abi was looking forward to celebrating her 28th birthday and was getting ready for a party that her friend had organised, to take place in a bar in the city of London.

It was a Saturday night in August and the city was in full bloom with flowing summer dresses and the scent of fine aftershave. Once she was in the bar, Abi spotted a gentleman smiling at her. The rest of the evening was spent dancing and talking with the handsome stranger.

A week later, the pair had made arrangements to meet each other at

Embankment station for a boat tour of London. 'Let's stop in Greenwich for some lunch?' Abi's new friend, Nii announced. After their first meal together they opted for dessert in Covent Garden.

Next was a day trip to Stratford-upon-Avon. As the weeks went on and more dates were arranged, one of Abi's friends noticed that she was spending more and more time in Nii's company. Abi reflected, 'it's the first time I've ever wanted to see someone, again and again! I feel totally myself with him and I don't feel I have to pretend to be someone else.'
The two of them sat and spoke it over, Nii said, 'doesn't it feel like we've known each other for much longer than just a few months?'
'It certainly does,' Abi agreed.
About a year and a half went by and Nii invited Abi to a formal, work evening event. He said, 'block out the whole evening in your diary Abi, and dress to impress, it's going to be a very important event.'

So Abi did as requested, looking forward to a night out. They were to meet at the same spot where they had their first date, Embankment. Upon arriving at the venue, Nii's colleagues were nowhere to be seen. Nii phoned his manager, 'ahh, you've moved onto another venue, alright then we'll meet you there,' Abi heard Nii say. En-route to the new location , right on the Embankment, next to the River Thames boat cruise, Nii got down on one knee, in front of tourists stopping to smile and clap, and proposed. It had all been a ruse!

Abi accepted and the two went straight onto the night cruiser for a celebratory dinner and dance. They were married the following year and then travels, with a honeymoon spent in Singapore, Malaysia and Indonesia. Shortly after the wedding, they spent three months working in New York before returning to north London to settle down and raise a family.

Abi's friend asked her one-day, 'what's the secret to a successful relationship?' 'Well,' replied Abi, I believe it's first realising that your life partner might not come in the package you first envisage; understanding each other's thoughts and values; lastly, it's accepting change, as the different seasons of marriage pass. Most importantly though, to treasure the fact that you've been given a best friend who 'has your back' for life.'

Paul and Laura

Paul and Laura are devoted to each other, sharing the other's tears of laughter and tears of sorrow. The two are a shining light of what it means to be patient and kind. They realise how lucky they are, to have found each other and were married on the 29th May 2015 at Casertavecchia Cathedral, with a reception party at Castel Campagnano, Italy.

When Paul saw Laura for the first time, it wasn't how Laura envisaged. The allure that should have been lost, upon seeing the young woman change from her flat shoes to her heels, on the street outside Electric Ballroom only intensified for the 32-year-old single man.

'It's her!' Paul couldn't take his eyes off her, 'she's even better in the flesh.' Now standing a good five inches taller, Laura pushed the battered ballet pumps to the bottom of her handbag, checked her reflection in the bar's lit-up window and applied some more lip gloss.

The 25-year-old woman, just a few feet away from him was not only stunning but she was also his date for the night. The pair had spotted each other's profile on the dating web site called mysinglefriend.com. The year was 2008 and society was just starting to accept that the internet was indeed the piazza of the present day, where the unattached could go to socialise and perhaps meet someone special.

When Paul then invited Laura out for a drink, the mademoiselle was so seized by nerves, that just before the date, she met a friend and downed half a bottle of fine red wine.

'It's for Dutch courage,' she assured her friend.

'Laura, you must text me as soon as you get a chance, to tell me what he's like, ok?'

'Definitely,' and with that, Laura was off to Old Street to meet Paul in person for the first time - inside Electric Ballroom. But he was waiting for her outside.

'Laura? It's me Paul,' said Paul with a beaming smile.

'Paul! Oh I thought you were going to meet me inside?' replied Laura, with a look of horror on her face. 'Did he just see me get ready for our date on the street? Oh the shame,' thought Laura.

'I thought you'd never find me in there, it's packed. Shall we go in together?' he asked, feeling pretty sure he did the right thing. But by the look on her face he now wasn't sure.

What followed was a bar-hopping, talk-a-thon tour which lasted beyond Laura's last train home. Furthermore, while she was in the taxi on her way home, they continued to speak on the phone. Before falling asleep that morning, the retail menswear buyer texted her friend as promised. She wrote, 'He dresses like he belongs in the Backstreet Boys but for once in my life I don't give a damn. I think he's really lovely!'

The couple embarked on a courtship which would take them to far-flung destinations together. Then, on Laura's 30th birthday Paul organised a wedding proposal, bending down on one knee, in the middle of St Mark's Square, in Venice. After crying, then laughing, high on happy emotions, Paul tried to coax Laura to a particular restaurant where he knew the whole family were waiting to congratulate the engagement (he had a feeling she was going to accept).

Salvatore and Gloria

S alvatore and Gloria are made for each other. Together they are described as 'really good people' and their many friends are testament of their delightful natures. They were married on the 7th July 1974 at St Peter's Italian Church in Clerkenwell. The couple have two children, Claudia and Giancarlo, and two grandchildren, Eleonora and Stefano.

B ack in the dawn of the 1970s, an Italian-French club existed in London's West End. Italians and French alike flocked to the London night spot to dance, have a drink and perhaps meet someone nice. Gloria and her sister had great fun, giving nick names to the various characters who struck-up conversation.

There was 'Bossy' who would command women to dance rather than ask. 'Still thinks he's in the Army,' Gloria concluded, while stubbing out a cigarette. Her sister agreed. Next there was 'Flash Harry', whose real name was

Salvatore, and he liked nothing more than buying drinks for people and being seen. 'What do you think of him?' asked Gloria's sister. 'Who, Flash Harry? Too young!' Salvatore approached them at this moment and offered them a drink. Nonetheless, when the evening's slow song came on, Tony Renis' Non Mi Dire Mai Goodbye, Salvatore asked Gloria to dance.

For their first date, Salvatore booked a table for two at a popular steak house. Gloria had never eaten at a restaurant in London before now and was both excited and nervous, not knowing what to expect. It was also the first time she had ever been out on a formal date. Gloria's niece, Eleonora was in town, a smart girl from Italy's Napoli region, who gave Gloria a stark warning, 'with men, if they give you something, they will want something in return'.

This piece of advice rang in Gloria's ears as she made her way to the restaurant. She honestly didn't believe this relationship would go anywhere. At the restaurant, Salvatore was waiting for her. He beamed upon seeing her and promptly began ordering. First came drinks, then he ordered starters. With each course Salvatore noticed that Gloria was becoming paler and a little withdrawn, not her usual sharp self. 'What's the matter? Are you not feeling well?'
'I, I, I'm not feeling well, that's right,' Gloria stammered. The truth was, Gloria saw that with each item ordered, Salvatore was going to expect something big in return! Isn't that what Eleonora had said? Salvatore asked for the bill and Gloria made her excuses and went home.

The pair continued to see each other. About a month later, it was time for Gloria to return to Italy, for good. Salvatore tried his best to make his feelings known but Gloria wasn't convinced. Back in Italy, in familiar surroundings, Gloria was eating at a restaurant one night, with her family, in Amalfi. Her brother asked her, 'so what about the Italian chap you met in London?'
'Who Salvatore? That was a joke. And keep your voice down, I don't want mum and dad finding out. Now let me listen to some good Italian music and forget about crazy London.'
The song, Non Mi Dire Mai Goodbye came on. Gloria looked up and to her amazement saw Salvatore standing before her. 'Did you forget the words to our song? (Don't Ever Tell Me Goodbye) - well, please, I'm asking you, please don't tell me goodbye again?' The couple were married the following year.

Zak and Jo

Zak and Josephine, who met at school, complement each other like pen and paper. They were married on the 5th August 2006 at St Joseph's Church in Waltham Cross. They have two children, Charlie and Sam. In 2016, the couple celebrate their 10th wedding anniversary, with a renewal of their vows on the island of Sicily.

It was the mid-1990s and if you attended any healthy secondary school in the land, you would have been in one of two groups of school children - either the academic group (otherwise referred to as 'the geeks') or the popular group (home to the not so academic pupils).

Zak belonged to the latter. All the popular lads counted him as their 'mate'. It was important for Zak to fit in, after-all, he had a 'rep to protect'. As the years rolled by, the boys' attention turned from mocking their peers, to *girls*. Zak had his eye on Josephine. However, being the attractive, dark-haired Sicilian that she was, Josephine already had a boyfriend.

Nonetheless, whenever Zak spotted Josephine in the common room, he was always friendly, saying hello and even making her smile with his rendition of the latest popular ballad in the charts. Josephine confided to a close friend one day, 'that Zak is a perfect gentleman if it wasn't for the group of attention-seekers that he's friends with. '

Zak had to wait a couple of years. The Class of 2000 had long celebrated the end of exams and the onset of summer but one night a few of them found themselves at Eros, a nightclub that used to stand on the A10 in Enfield, amongst warehouses and outlets.

Zak saw Josephine with her friends and everyone was drinking more than they should. Zak gathered all the confidence he could muster, and when the moment was right, kissed Josephine. When he asked for her number, a tipsy Josephine gave it to him.

The following day Zak was both buzzing with excitement and terrified at the possibility that she didn't feel the same way. He needn't have worried, the two met up the following day and when they held hands Zak knew that they definitely had a connection.

The two were inseparable. A few years after that and Zak was planning the engagement. 'Ring? Check. Ask father-in-law to be? Check. All that's left is book somewhere posh for dinner!' said a contented Zak to himself.

He had it all planned. Earlier he had told Paulo, Josephine's father, 'when Jo's not looking, I'll slip the ring into the champagne flute, I pour the champagne and while Jo attempts to drink it, she sees the ring. At that moment I drop to one knee and ask her!' In reality, Josephine told Zak that she didn't fancy a chic supper that night and instead opted for their local Chinese restaurant, on Cheshunt High Street.

As they sat down, the restaurant manager noticed something different about his two young regulars, 'why do you want Champagne, Zak,' he asked. 'Are you getting engaged?' So an impromptu plan B entailed a startled Zak, pouring Jo a lukewarm flute of champagne, sliding the ring-box across the table and saying, 'put that on your finger because we're getting married!' And to his utter delight, Jo said 'Yes!'

Epilogue

At Marriage Care we believe that men and women from all walks of life and spiritual experiences are capable of catching a glimpse of something beautiful and hopeful, even divine, in the possibilities of marriage and family life. As one of our clients about to embark on marriage said, marriage is a journey.

This book, written by Natasha Collins, is about the beginning of 16 love journeys into marriage capturing the excitement and fun of their love for each other but also showing us a glimpse of the journeys since then. As these stories also hint, happy marriages don't just happen: they require regular investment and maintenance.

Remembering that initial love and joy in each other can help to give couples who are struggling, hope that their love in each other can be rekindled.

As our name suggests we care deeply about marriage and offering relationship support for couples at all stages of their journey together, in the good times and the tough times too – and we've been doing so for nearly 70 years.

Our marriage preparation services delivered by our fantastic volunteers help couples to nurture faithful and fruitful marriages that will last. Our qualified and accredited volunteer counsellors offer professional support for those whose love journey is hard and we dare to hope that even the most fragile of relationships can be rebuilt and strengthened. We are grateful to Natasha for offering some of the proceeds from this book celebrating love to help us in our support of marriage and couple relationships.

Mark Molden, Chief Executive Marriage Care

marriage
care

better relationships
better lives

Marriage Care is the largest faith-based provider of relationship support services in the UK and we provide marriage and relationship information, education and counselling to thousands of people each year through our network of centres and professionally trained and accredited volunteers.

For further information about Marriage Care go to:
www.marriagecare.org.uk